Topsy and Tim were going to stay
the night with Tony Welch. They
were very excited. It would be their
first night away from Mummy and Dad.

They made two big piles of clothes
and toys on the floor. Mummy gave
them each a zip-up bag. 'You won't
need to take all that,' she said.
'You're only going for one night.'

Topsy + Tim

stay with a friend

Jean and Gareth Adamson

Blackie

British Library Cataloguing in Publication Data
Adamson, Jean, 1928—
Topsy and Tim stay with a friend
I. Title   II. Adamson, Gareth, 1925–1982
823'.914 [J]

ISBN 0-216-93133-9
ISBN 0-216-93132-0 Pbk

Blackie and Son Limited
7 Leicester Place
London WC2H 7BP

Printed in Hong Kong by
Wing King Tong Co. Ltd.

Topsy and Tim started all over again.
They packed their washing things and
toothbrushes, their pyjamas and some
clean clothes.

'I wish we could take Kitty with us,'
said Topsy.
'And Roly Poly,' said Tim.

'Why don't you take your dear old
teddies?' said Mummy.
'No,' said Tim. 'Tony will think we're
babies if we take our teddies to bed
with us.'
'Well, I'm taking mine,' said Topsy.

When they were ready, Dad took them
to Tony's house. Tony and his
mum were waiting for them.

'Come and see where you're going
to sleep,' said Tony.
They all raced upstairs.
'Bye. Be good,' Dad called after them.

There was a camp bed in Tony's room,
next to Tony's bed.
'That's your bed, Tim,' said Tony.
'Where's my bed?' asked Topsy.

'Here,' said Tony, jumping onto a
mattress on the floor.
'Lucky you,' said Tim. They all started
to bounce on Topsy's bed. It made
a good trampoline. Tony's mum
heard the noise and came upstairs.
'Tea's ready,' she said.

Tony's mum gave them their favourite tea.
'It's like a party,' said Topsy.
'It is a party,' said Tony.

After tea, Topsy and Tim and Tony went out to play football in the garden.

Then they took turns to ride Tony's
bike. When it was Tim's turn, Topsy
didn't want to get off the bike.
Tim gave her a push. Topsy
wobbled and fell off and the bike
fell on top of her.
'Ow! Ow! Ow!' cried Topsy.

Tony's mum came running to see
what was wrong.
'I want my mummy,' sobbed Topsy.
Tony's mum gave her a cuddle and
soon she felt better.

'It's nearly bedtime,' said Tony's mum.
'Would you like the first bath, Topsy?'
She gave Topsy a warm, bubbly bath
and helped her into her pyjamas.

Then Tony's mum called the boys in.
They were rather muddy.
'We've had a lovely time,' said Tim.
'I can see you have,' said Tony's mum.
Tony and Tim took turns in the shower.

When Tony's mum came to tuck them up
in bed, Tony was lying down, cuddling
his big, old teddy bear.
Tim was sitting up and he didn't
look happy at all.
'Are you all right, Tim?' asked
Tony's mum.

'I want to go home,' said Tim.
'Oh, dear,' said Tony's mum.
'I think you are feeling
homesick.'

Topsy got out of bed and came to cheer
Tim up. She was cuddling her dear old
teddy.
'I wish I'd brought my teddy,' said Tim.
'You have,' said Tony's mum. 'He's
in your bag.'
'Mummy must have packed him after all,'
said Topsy.

Soon Topsy and Tim and Tony were all tucked up with their dear old teddies beside them.

'Sleep well,' said Tony's mum. 'We'll have lots more fun tomorrow.'

After Tony's mum had gone downstairs,
Tony said, 'I don't feel like going
to sleep.'
Topsy and Tim didn't feel sleepy either.
Soon they were having a lovely game of
rabbit burrows in the beds.

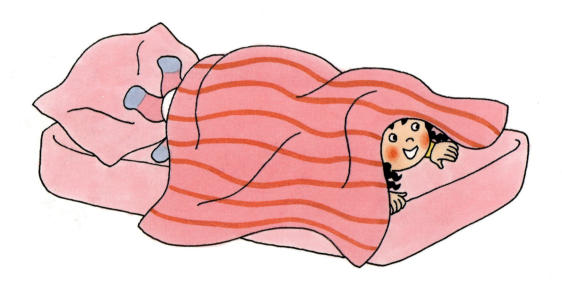

When Tony's mum looked in later that night, Tony's bedroom was in a mess but Topsy and Tim and Tony were all fast asleep. And their teddies were, too.